———— PRAISE FOR ————

# Scallywag on t

"Young pirate fans will relish every vivid and revolting detail as they root for the hero of this hilarious romp. The concise language is as keen as a scallywag's cutlass, and the words are perfectly matched by the comical illustrations."

**Kit Pearson** author of *Be My Love*

"A fun, absurd, and satisfying story. Kids will laugh out loud at the goofy humour and will enjoy getting to know this resourceful young hero and motley crew of tough-but-sweet pirates."

**Robin Stevenson** author of *Kid Activists* and *Ghost's Journey*

"From the sweet weevils and chewy maggots to the clever gulls and intrigue, this page-turning tale has just the right blend of curdled humour and swashbuckling mystery."

**Aidan Cassie** author of *Sterling, Best Dog Ever*

"A rollicking, high-seas adventure full of humour and heart! With a hero who's easy to root for going up against a fearsome—and charmingly illustrated—crew of pirates, you'll be turning pages quicker than you can say 'scallywag.'"

**Gareth Wronski** author of *Holly Farb and the Princess of the Galaxy*

"A gem from out of the deep, this book is required reading for anyone in danger of being gambled away to pirates. Funny and tender and keen as a cutlass."

**John Gould** author of *Kilter: 55 Fictions*

"A pirate ship is no place for a young orphan boy, unless your boss gambles you away. With his heart set on finding out who he is and where he comes from, Kitch shows the reader how words and wit are mightier than pirates who sail the Salish Sea. This humorous story is packed with puns, pirate action, a supportive seagull, and some treasure, and is a fun tale to read aloud."

**Sarah Harrison** Middle Childhood & Tween Literacy Librarian,
Greater Victoria Public Library

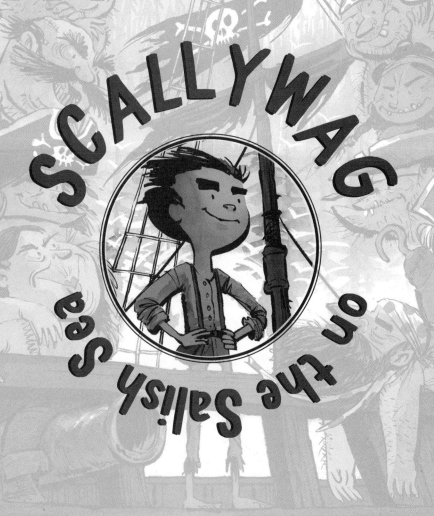

# SCALLYWAG
## on the Salish Sea

Sara Cassidy    Illustrations by Mike Deas

WANDERING FOX

An imprint of
HERITAGE HOUSE PUBLISHING
Victoria | Vancouver | Calgary

Wandering Fox Books
An imprint of Heritage House Publishing Company Ltd.
heritagehouse.ca

*Cataloguing information available from Library and Archives Canada*

978-1-77203-278-9 (pbk)
978-1-77203-291-8 (ebook)

Edited by Lara Kordic
Cover and interior book design by Jacqui Thomas

The interior of this book was produced on 100% post-consumer recycled paper, processed chlorine free and printed with vegetable-based inks.

Heritage House gratefully acknowledges that the land on which we live and work is within the traditional territories of the Lkwungen (Esquimalt and Songhees), Malahat, Pacheedaht, Scia'new, T'Sou-ke, and W̱SÁNEĆ (Pauquachin, Tsartlip, Tsawout, Tseycum) Peoples.

We acknowledge the financial support of the Government of Canada through the Canada Book Fund (CBF) and the Canada Council for the Arts, and the Province of British Columbia through the British Columbia Arts Council and the Book Publishing Tax Credit.

23 22 21 20 19  1 2 3 4 5

Printed in Canada

## CHAPTER ONE

"Ha! Ho! Hooo!" Captain Gallows whoops until the mainsails quiver and my kneecaps quake. His onion breath stings my eyes. "No wonder Billy didn't bawl when he lost you in that dice game. You're skinnier than a manrope. Got less muscle than a string bean. How could you be any help to *me*?"

"I p-peel p-potatoes," I stammer.

"I'd think a p-p-p-potato could p-p-p-peel *you*," says the captain, imitating me.

The pirates laugh. They slap their thighs and stomp their pegs, putting little round dents in the ship's deck. They howl until they cry, wiping

the tears from their eyes with their long greasy hair.

Gallows cuts the air with his ragged sword and everyone goes quiet. Everyone except for a seagull squawking on the topmast. She sounds like she's laughing at us all.

"I hate potatoes," Captain Gallows spits. "I was raised on the nasty things. Ate them for breakfast, lunch, supper, and beddy-bye snack. Potatoes, potatoes, potatoes, that's all we ever had. Fried, boiled, roasted, mashed, puréed, baked, boiled, fried—"

A coal-smudged pirate nudges a pirate on his left who looks just like him and whispers, "He said fried twice!"

"No, he didn't. He said *boiled* twice."

"Fried."

"Boiled."

"Fried."

"Silence!" Captain Gallows growls. "Listen up! My christening gown was a potato sack. My crib was a potato box. I spent my boyhood bent in a sandy field, planting, weeding, hilling, watering, weeding, hilling, and digging up dirty potatoes."

The coal-smudged pirate nudges his twin again. "He said hilling twice."

"No, he didn't. He said *weeding* twice."

"Hilling."

"Weeding."

"Shut it!" shouts the captain. "I'm telling you, mateys, potatoes is why I ran away to sea. I still get nightmares about them terrible tubers. In my baddest dreams I find a treasure chest with pretty flowers painted on the lid—"

"Pretty flowers?" teases a pirate who is missing an ear. "Aw, the captain likes things pretty."

"Skulls, I mean," the captain growls.

"*Pretty* skulls?" the pirate with one ear jibes.

"Ugly skulls. Like yours, One Ear!" The captain points a finger at his one good eye, then swings his hand around to point at One Ear. "I'm watching you," he warns. He clears his throat. "In my nightmare I pry the lid off with my trusty prosthetic." Captain Gallows breathes on his hook and buffs it on his filthy waistcoat. "Now, what do you think is inside the chest?"

"Rubies?" the pirates shout. "Emeralds?"

"No," the captain says. "The chest is full of terrifying, traumatizing *taters*. Soggy rocks! I wake up whimpering. Caterwauling and boo-hoo-hoo-ing. Snivelling and sobbing. Blubbering and—"

"The men are losing confidence, Captain," One Ear mumbles.

"Right. What I'm saying is potatoes are my enemies. So you, little boy, won't be p-p-peeling any of them for m-m-me."

I can't imagine not eating potatoes. "What do you eat, then?"

"Well, I quite like the toad crab, that hard-shelled scavenger of the dying and dead. And my palate is partial to sharp-nose shark. Matter of fact, I crunch the sharkey's bones like candies."

"Sharks don't actually h-have bones," I say. Grandma told me so. Of course, she wasn't really my grandma. "They've got cartilage instead, which is light and bendy and heals faster than—"

Captain Gallows bores into me with his one eye. "Enough! I won't take any edeecated guff from a thread like you. I—"

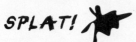
*SPLAT!*

A sloppy meringue of bird guano splatters onto the captain's tricorn hat.

The captain shakes his hook at the bird.

The bird just cackles and caws.

## CHAPTER TWO

Skullcap, the ship's cook, is as wide as he is tall and as bald as a seagull's egg. I try not to stare at the thick white line that runs across his forehead.

"Scar," Skullcap blurts, catching me trying not to look. "Goes all the way around. Well, nearly. There's a hinge, like."

"Oh," I say. I picture the top of his head flopped over like the lid of a treasure chest. "Oh."

Skullcap rubs the back of his head where I imagine the hinge is, then points at a heap of fish in the corner of the dark kitchen. "We got a nice catch today. A full net of wormy pollock. Your job, lad, is to cut off the heads and clean out the guts."

"Yuck."

"What's that?"

"Aye aye."

"If I give you a sharp knife, will you stab me in the back?"

"Of course not!"

Skullcap sighs. "Not even a little bit pirate, are you? Well, at least I know I'm safe with you. Here, catch."

Skullcap flings a knife across the kitchen. I jump out of the way just in time.

"*Oof!*" breathes a voice behind me.

I swing around. A pirate with two peg legs is doubled over and wincing behind me. The knife blade is lodged in his thigh!

"I'm sorry," I say. "I—I—"

The pirate grins. His gold teeth glint. He wiggles the knife out of his leg. I wait for blood to soak through his pantaloons, but there is none. He knocks on his thigh: tock. "Red oak. Right up to my hip. Sure, I wanted Madagascar Rosewood, but it's expensive and Captain is more miserly than sea lice. Never pays the doubloons he owes."

"Meet the new kitchen boy," Skullcap says. He turns to me. "Boy, this is Peggy."

"Peggy?" I ask. I know a Peggy: the barmaid at the Duncan Arms, who brought me tea sweetened with honey every night. "Is—is that short for Margaret?"

Peggy the pirate grabs me by the collar and lifts me off the ground. I hear my shirt stitches tear, and the top button pops off and rolls under the stove. "If I was named Margaret, do you think I'd go by the nickname Peggy?" He drops me to the dirty floor and strokes his gnarly beard. "I'd go with Meg."

"I'd choose Maggie, I think," Skullcap puts in.

"I would have thought you two would choose Margie," I say. "You know, M-*aaargh*-ie?"

Peggy grabs me by the collar again. More stitches rip. A second button rolls under the stove. "Are you making fun of us?"

"N-never," I squeak.

"For your information, I am called Peggy because I have got two peg legs, which makes me peggy, you know? I didn't used to be called Peggy. My name was in fact Epaphroditus Cuthbert Zebediah Habbakuk Bartholomew Wiley. But for some reason people can never remember that."

Peggy turns to Skullcap. "Heard you caught a full net today," he says. "How are the eyes?"

"They look good, Peggy."

"I wouldn't imagine they look at all," I say.

Peggy and Skullcap look at me funny.

"Ha ha?" I say.

"It's *har har*, boy," Peggy tells me.

"Har har," I try.

"Better." Peggy turns to Skullcap. "I'll give you my week's grog for them."

"The lad's cleaning the fish today. He's too young for grog."

"What'll you take?" Peggy asks me.

"F-for what?"

"He wants you to pluck out enough fish eyes to fill a jar," Skullcap explains.

My stomach heaves. Then I spy my shirt buttons under the stove, glittering like, well, like a pair of fish eyes. "I'll do it for a needle and thread."

"Can the needle be dull and rusty?"

"No!"

"I've only got a dull and rusty one."

"Sharpen it, Peggy," Skullcap says.

Later, Skullcap explains that an herbalist told Peggy that eating fish eyes would make his legs grow back.

"That's ridiculous," I say.

"I know. But he believes it. And I've gotten a lot of grog out of it. And you'll now have a needle and thread."

I don't answer. I'm entranced by a scar I hadn't noticed earlier on Skullcap's neck.

"That one goes all the way around, too," Skullcap says. "Nearly."

"H-hinge?"

"Yep. Life was tough before I became a pirate."

"Wh-what did you do?"

"I was a tax collector."

## CHAPTER THREE

**S**kullcap places a three-legged stool in the middle of the pile of pollock and hands me another knife and a strange spoon with tip that's jagged like a saw.

"My invention," Skullcap explains. "Makes it easy to dig out the eye. Just fling it against the wall there. You'll soon build up a nice pile."

"This spoon would work well for eating grapefruit."

"Grapefruit? Never heard of it." Skullcap pinches his earlobes. "Blast, it's cold."

Flinging fish eyes is actually fun, but the wormy pollock is slimy and disgusting.

"There's a song to make your work go quicker," Skullcap says. "Listen."

You don't clean a fish with soap—nope!
This isn't time for hope—nope!
Clear the belly, guts and jelly...
THUMP-thump.
What's that sound?
THUMP-thump.
The heart still pounds!
Sharpen your blade, don't be afraid.
Cut off the head—ho!
Now it's dead—oh.

How I miss the Duncan Arms. Even though I didn't get paid much for working there, and my bed was lumpy as poor man's porridge, at least the floor didn't rock beneath me, and when people laughed there wasn't meanness in it.

Also, I felt that my parents could walk in any day. Not here. No one just appears on a ship.

The Duncan Arms is a tavern on Vancouver Island on the edge of the Salish Sea. I worked there for two years until my boss gambled me away in a game of dice. Billy McCobben is a good man when he's sober. But when he's drunk, which he often is, he doesn't think straight. I'm not angry, though. After all, he took me in when I was alone in the world. It was the second time I'd been alone in the world.

The first time, I was just a baby, lying on the highway outside of Ladysmith, crying at the blue sky above me. Or maybe I was cooing, I don't know. What I know is someone saved me. She or he wrapped me in a green felt hat and laid me on the doorstep of a farmhouse. They attached a note to the hat:

This baby fell from a carriage that was being chased by wild boars.

The old couple that lived at the house took me in, and I came to call them Grandma and Grandpa. But when I was eight, I was out picking blueberries three meadows over when I smelled smoke on the breeze. I dropped my berry basket and ran as fast as I could. When I reached the old couple's house, two fire brigadiers, their faces covered with kerchiefs, carried the old couple out on stretchers. One of them said Grandma and Grandpa had breathed in too much smoke.

"What about the boy?" the other asked.

I ducked behind a bush. Hot tears stung my cheeks.

"What boy?"

"The boy what lived here. Who will look after him with these two dead?"

"Orphanage, I expect."

No orphanage for me! I crashed out of the bushes and flew.

"Whoa! Boy!" the brigadiers yelled. But I was already gone.

I didn't stop running. I propelled myself across fields and through forests and along rivers, crying and sobbing for the old couple that had taken me in as a baby and loved me. I napped in fields with snuffling marmots, shivered long nights in barns with scurrying shrews. I bathed at the ocean's edge while steelhead salmon and

striped dolphins leapt around me as if trying to cheer me up.

Once, I spent the night in the back of a dairy truck, my mattress a block of cheddar, my pillow a sack of curds. I confess I ate a few bites of that pillow. I was starving. But maybe that's why I'm on this pirate ship now—because I thieved.

After seven nights sleeping wild, I reached Duncan, where I stumbled down the main road, hungry and filthy as a chimney sweep. Through the window of a tavern, a woman sang about three ravens. Her voice was like a dark, thick river that lulled me to sleep right there on the tavern's woodpile.

When I awoke, I had been moved to a lumpy mattress in a clanging place. A cup of sweet tea steamed on a barrel beside my modest bed. I was in the busy kitchen of the Duncan Arms, where I would spend the next two years as kitchen boy. That's what they called me: Kitchen Boy, and, eventually, just Kitch.

I don't know my real name. Grandma was too superstitious to give me one. She thought it would be like a curse against me ever finding my parents. Instead of a name, she and Grandpa called me Dear, Little One, Love, and especially Sweetheart. For a long time, I thought my name *was* Sweetheart.

Then Grandma and Grandpa died, and I crossed valleys and forests and met Peggy, the barmaid at the Duncan Arms. "Goodnight, Kitch," she'd say each night, kissing my forehead three times.

Then, after two years of peeling potatoes all day and drinking sweet tea each night, my boss Billy McCobben, sailing two sheets to the wind (that means he was stumbling drunk on rum), gambled me in a game of cards.

Now here I am. Seasick, flinging slimy pollock eyes at a dirty galley wall.

## CHAPTER FOUR

I yank about a dozen hearts from a dozen dead pollock when I feel a heart unlike the others. It's large and hard as stone. I separate it carefully from the fish guts and hold it up in the thin stream of light that pierces the dirty kitchen window. The heart is shiny and red. It glows!

Only it's not a heart. It's a jewel! I tuck it into my purse. Then I find the fish's real heart—soft, ugly, grey—and drop it into the bucket with the others.

I look very carefully now when I clean each fish. As I work through the pollock, I find two more red jewels. I think maybe they're rubies.

Then I come upon a fish with a hard, bright green liver. An emerald!

Then an eye clicks when it hits the wall. Until now the eyes have only gone shplat. I roll up my sleeve and swish my hand around in the mushy mound of eyeballs.

"What are you doing?" Skullcap asks.

"Lost something," I say.

"Your marbles, perchance?"

My hand closes on something small and sharp.

It's mucky with eyeball juice, but it glitters. I think it's a diamond.

In all, I find three rubies, three emeralds, and two diamonds. I put them into the small leather pouch I keep tied to my belt. I'm wiping my hands on my apron when *BANG!*

"Captain's quarters," grunts Skullcap, pointing to the ceiling. "If he drops his cannonball once, it means he's hungry. Twice, he wants grog. Three times, we're under attack."

"A-attack?"

"Yes, attack. This ain't no carousel ride," Skullcap says. The ship lurches, sending me crashing against a rum barrel. "Though it can feel like one."

Skullcap hands me a plate with three grey lumps. "Take this to the captain."

"What is it?"

"Hard tack washed of mould. Scoop of sauerkraut. And a sloppy slab of boiled pollock."

"Which is which?"

"Your guess is as good as mine, boy."

Skullcap asks me to dump the fish heads overboard while I'm up on deck. As soon as I do, the seagull that earlier squawked at the captain swoops in and gulps them down. "Bon appétit, Meringue," I call to her. We always said "bon appétit" to the diners at the Duncan Arms. It's fancy for "Enjoy your meal."

As Meringue flaps away, a strand of dulse works loose from her feathers and falls to the deck. It's the kind we used to add to the chowder at the Duncan Arms. I curl it into the shape of a rose and place it on the edge of the captain's plate. I'm about to climb the three stairs to the captain's cabin when a pirate with black teeth jumps in my way.

"I've got your purse," she sneers.

My hand flies to my belt.

The pirate dangles my leather pouch in my face, then tosses it to the pirate twins, saying, "Catch, boys!"

"Yo ho!" the twins gabble. They toss my purse back and forth between them. "Yo ho!"

"Give it!" I shout.

But the twins don't stop. "Har har!" they laugh in unison.

The black-toothed pirate snarls, "Pass it to me now."

The twins keep throwing it back and forth between them. "We're stuck," cries one. "In a loop."

The mean-looking pirate flashes a knife at me. "The name's Cut-Purse," she tells me.

"I-I can guess wh-why they call you that," I say, fingering the purse strings on my belt. I nod toward the twins. "What are *their* names?"

"Jolly and Roger."

"Which is which?"

"No one knows. Not even them. What's in that purse, anyway? Stones from home to remember Mommy by? Aw."

Just then the purse smacks Cut-Purse on the side of the head and falls to the deck.

"It got unstuck!" Jolly and Roger cheer.

"Curse ye!" Cut-Purse seethes. She reaches for the purse. "Now, let's take a look…"

"No!" I cry. "You're right; they're pebbles from home."

"We'll see about that."

"No!"

**CAW! CAW!**

Meringue swoops in from out of the sky. She knocks Cut-Purse over with a big dirty wing, then grabs my purse in her beak.

"Well done, Meringue!" I yell.

Meringue flies farther and farther away. My heart drops as she shrinks against the grey sky.

Moments ago, I was the richest kitchen boy in the world.

Now, I'm nothing again.

Nothing but me.

## CHAPTER FIVE

Captain Gallows is at his desk, writing numbers in a ledger. He sniffles, and a tear runs down his dirty cheek.

"You all right, Captain?" I ask.

"Allergies," he grunts. "Aye. I'm allergic to being broke."

I wipe down a small table with the corner of my shirt, shine his spoon on the edge of a dirty curtain, and carry a candle over from his bedside.

"Timbers! Aren't we fancy?" the captain says, sitting to his meal. His nose wrinkles. "What's the vegetabley stuff?"

"Petal weed, sir. Tasty. Good for you, too."

"I like things that are *bad* for me, boy. This grey pile here—it's not potatoes, is it? I *hate* potatoes. I was raised on them—"

"It's not potatoes. You've got sauerkraut, pollock, and tack."

"Which is which?"

"No one can say."

As Gallows digs into his meal, I peek at his ledger. I don't know my numbers, but I know what zero is, and this ledger has lots of them.

*TAP-TAP. TAP-TAP.*

"What in tarnation?" the captain asks.

It's Meringue! She's tapping at the porthole, with my purse still in her beak. I unhook the window latch. Meringue mews as I reach out. "It's all right," I whisper.

She drops my purse into my hand. "Thank you for saving it," I say.

Meringue lets me stroke her head. It's soft—soft as, well, feathers.

"Shut the blasted window!" Gallows shouts. "You're letting the heat out." He rubs his hands together and whimpers, "We're nearly out of coal. And I've got no doubloons to buy more."

Perfect!

"I can help you," I tell the captain. "I can get you enough coal to last for years."

"Skinny little you?" the captain snorts. He goes back to slurping down his supper. He looks me over again. "And how would I pay for it?"

"With my freedom."

Gallows looks me over. He scratches his head. Small flakes fall into his plate. "I don't make deals with galley boys," he snarls finally. He spoons a lump of grey food into his mouth.

"Fine, then. Bon appétit," I say and turn to leave. But as I exit the door something thumps me in the back. Gallows has thrown his boot at me! "What the—?" I ask, looking back. The captain's face is redder than a ruby. His hands grip his throat. He points desperately at a pair of silver tweezers on his desk.

"You want me to yank that awful hair from your nostril?" I ask. "Is that it?"

The captain shakes his head. He wheezes. His one eye bulges. I know what's wrong. This kind of thing happened sometimes at the Duncan Arms. But I keep Gallows waiting for an extra minute. I make him suffer a little. Maybe the pirate life is rubbing off on me!

"You want me to pick lice out of your beard?" I ask.

The captain shakes his big ugly head. He points to his neck.

"Pop that big pimple?"

The captain pounds his good fist on the table, making his plate and spoon dance. He shakes his head again.

"I've got it!" I say. "You've got a fish bone stuck in your throat."

The captain sputters and nods.

"And if I remove it, and then lead you to a load of coal, you'll release me from your service?"

The captain rolls his one eye angrily, opens his mouth wide, and tips back his head. I take the silver tweezers and reach past the black nubs of his molars, through the thick, bad breath, and pinch the offending pollock bone. I pull.

Within minutes, the captain is breathing normally and listening carefully to the skinny kitchen boy that he won in a dice game telling him the miraculous story of treasure discovered in a pile of dead fish.

"There must be a pile of jewels near where those fish were caught," I finish. "Maybe even a treasure chest. Enough jewels to buy ten ship-loads of coal."

"To the wheelhouse!" Gallows thunders. He stands, then immediately falls. "Curses! Forgot I took off my leg." He straps on his leg and stands again. "Okay, now. To the wheelhouse! We've got to turn this ship hard about."

When he's at the cabin door, he stops and looks me over carefully. I think he's going to thank me. For saving his life, or for steering him toward treasure. But, no. "You were right, boy. Petal weed is kinda tasty."

He fixes his eye on me again.

"What is it?" I ask.

"I don't know," Gallows says, squinting. "Have we met before?"

"I think I'd remember that."

"Yessir. I am memorable, all right. Arrgh! I'm the meanest pirate east of Gambier Island."

"Actually, we're west of Gambier…"

## CHAPTER SIX

On deck, Peggy pours the fish eyes down his throat. My stomach churns.

Peggy wipes his mouth and belches, then squeezes the top of his leg. "It's growing back," he whispers excitedly.

"That's good," I say.

"Here. I sharpened the needle and filched some thread from a mainsail."

The ship suddenly lurches. Pirates skid and topple across the deck. The ship is being turned hard around. The sharpened sewing needle flies from my hand.

"It's all right!" Peggy calls from where he has landed in a pile of rigging. He points at his oaken thigh: there is my needle, thrust like Excalibur in the stone.

"What's so good about that pollock that the captain would change course for it?" Skullcap asks as he carves rot from a leg of salted pork. He shakes his scarred head. "Something's up."

I hate keeping a secret from Skullcap, but the captain forbade me to talk about the jewels until he meets with the crew.

Skullcap has strung two hammocks across the kitchen for us to sleep in. I'm cross-legged in mine, sewing the buttons back onto my shirt and my purse strings back onto my purse.

Skullcap finishes his work and, without washing his hands or even taking off his boot, climbs into his hammock.

He bowls his hands over his mouth and blows. "It's hard to fall asleep when it's this freezing."

"I could sing to you," I say.

"Pirates don't sing lullabies."

"I'm not a pirate," I remind him.

Skullcap nestles deeper into his hammock. "Go on, then."

Our hammocks swing in time as I remember the song I heard that first day in Duncan:

> There were three ravens sat on a tree.
> Down a down, hey down, hey down.
> They were as black as black can be.

> Then one of them said to his mate,
> "Where shall we our breakfast take?"
> With a down, derry, derry, derry,
> down, down.

"Get up early to make breakfast..." Skullcap mumbles groggily. "Thick, sticky, lumpy porridge..."

> Down in yonder green field
> Down a down, hey down, hey down...

As Skullcap snores, I finish my mending, then lay my own head down to sleep. For a pillow, I've stuffed a kitchen apron into my green felt hat. As I doze off, I finger the rubies, emeralds, and diamonds in my leather pouch.

I'm rich! And soon I'll be free.

## CHAPTER SEVEN

*BANG. BANG. BANG. BANG.*

**S**kullcap bolts upright. "Cap'n wants his grog?"

"He dropped the cannonball *four* times!" I say.

Skullcap's scars turn pink "*Four* times?! Shiver me timbers, we're damned to the depths!"

"What does four times mean?"

"I don't know."

As we struggle out of our hammocks like fish wriggling from a net, Jolly and Roger appear at the galley door.

"We're being followed!"

"By each other?" Skullcap asks.

"I don't think so!"

Jolly (or Roger) turns to his brother. "Are you following me?"

"Of course not," Roger (or Jolly) answers. "Are you following me?"

"Why would I do that?"

"Come to think of it, you're always near. Ever since we was laddies. Ever since we was born. Mommy said you came out right behind me. You *are* following me!"

"I am not! You're just always ahead of me."

The twins start pushing each other. "Back off."

"I'll back off when you back off."

"Ahoy!"

"Argh!"

"Avast!"

"Arrr!"

"Scallywags! Enough!" Skullcap hollers. "Why are you here?"

"Right," says Jolly/Roger. "Gallows wants everyone on deck."

"Tell him we'll be up after we put the porridge on."

"Right. Let's go, Brother."

"I'm right behind you."

The captain squats on a bollard, whittling a stick. By the time everyone is on deck, he has carved a fine toothpick, which he uses to dig something grey and wriggling from between his teeth. He shows it off. "Maggot. From the tack, no doubt."

"Oooh," say the pirates. "Chubby!"

The captain returns the maggot to his mouth, chews, and swallows. My stomach lifts into my throat.

But I'm thinking about that toothpick. I've seen one like it before.

"The news is this, mateys," the captain starts. "I turned the ship around last night."

"Aye, I felt that," says Peggy, rubbing his head.

"We're headed back to the banks where we caught that delicious pollock. My belly needs more."

"I'm a pirate, not a fisherman," Cut-Purse grumbles.

"Thing is," the captain continues. He pulls a telescope from his boot and takes a long look across the sea. "It looks like that sudden turn called us some attention. That enemy ship has been riding our wake all night."

"M-maybe they just want to s-say hello," I suggest.

Captain Gallows ignores me. "If it comes any closer, we attack. Jolly and Roger, you remember the recipe for fire arrows?"

"We sure do."

Jolly and Roger link arms, kick up their legs, and sing:

Saltpeter, gunpowder, brimstone—

mix them up with oil.

Fill a little pillow, tie it to an arrow,

let your enemies howl!

"You others, ready the arrows and keep an eye on that ship," Captain Gallows orders.

"Aye aye!"

"Sir," I say. "What about—"

"You. I need your help lowering the nets for that pollock."

"No. What about the—"

"Porridge? You're right. Breakfast first."

"No, I mean the jewel—"

The captain grabs me by the collar. I've sewn the buttons on well. "Boy, you speak when you're asked to speak."

"B-but—"

The Captain lifts me higher and hisses in my ear, "If I tell the men about the jewels now, they'll start celebrating. Nothing gets done when pirates are happy, you hear?"

"O-oh," I say.

## CHAPTER EIGHT

"It's sticking to the bottom!" I shout. "Add more water."

"Barnacles, you're fussy," Skullcap says. "Never saw anyone dress up porridge. Cinnamon and raisins and sugar and a pinch of nutmeg?"

I give him a taste from the wooden spoon and his eyes light up. "Aren't you the chef?"

"Skullcap, I've got to tell you something."

"Is it a secret?"

"Yes."

"I'm bad at keeping secrets."

"It's the kind you can tell."

"I'm good with that kind."

"There's treasure at the pollock banks."

"*Treasure?*"

"Rubies, emeralds, diamonds. I found some in the fish. I told Gallows. He was supposed to tell everyone, but—"

"Why, that rabid, sharkey-eating blighter!"

"He says he's going make an announcement."

"Like bilge water, he is!"

Over breakfast, Skullcap gathers the others. I fill their bowls over and over as they whisper up a plan. They love the porridge. They lick the pot clean. Literally.

I deliver a bowl to Captain Gallows. "There's weevils in this porridge," he says. "The sweetest weevils I ever tasted."

"Those are raisins."

"Never heard of them." As he gobbles down his porridge, the captain tells me his own plan.

"Once we're at the pollock banks, I'll lower you over the side of the ship in a net."

"But I'll freeze!"

"Well, you wanted to get *free*. *Free*-zing? Har har."

"When will you tell the others about the jewels?"

"It's like this, laddie: they don't really have to know. You and I can share the booty. There's more that way."

One Ear appears at the door. "I've dropped anchor, sir. The net's ready."

"Good."

Gallows digs his sword into my back. "One Ear gets a share, too. He's my most trusty pirate. Now go." Gallows steers me to the back of the ship and forces me onto the net laid out on the deck. He directs One Ear to lower me overboard.

Below, the ocean churns with froth. I scream, but my voice is lost on the wind. I wriggle as the net gets closer to the water.

I scream again. Something screeches back! It's Meringue! She's heard me. She swoops in and starts pecking at Gallows's ugly face and beats his head with her big wings.

One Ear jerks the net up, and before I know what's happening I land back on the deck with a thud.

Gallows pulls out his pistol and aims it at Meringue.

"No!" I scream, freeing myself from the net.

A flash of colour catches my eye. A pirate in a red jacket with brass buttons, cutlass glinting and braids flying, is *cartwheeling* along the ship railing towards us! "Halloo-oo!" he sings, coming to a stop right behind Gallows.

Gallows swings around. His eye bulges out. "Heinous Henry! That's *your* ship what's been following us?"

"That's right, Greggory Gallows. What's it been? Ten years since we last saw each other?"

"Ten years since you left me stranded on a country road," Gallows replies.

"With a baby cooing in your arms. You were so … paternal."

"I had pity."

"A pirate with pity ain't no pirate, Greggory."

Captain Gallows charges at Heinous. "That baby was innocent." He turns toward One Ear and me. "This scurvy dog and I were robbing a carriage when he kidnapped one of its passengers and tossed her baby into the roadside grass."

"Boo-hoo," Heinous Henry teases. "That lady blubbered for her baby for days and nights. She turned out to be a wonderful cook, though.

Ran the galley for three years on the *Diabla Maria*. Ran away after talking me into docking in Ganges to get some bakeapples. Said she needed them badly for a pie recipe. I'm a sucker for pie, and I didn't see the ruse ..."

Heinous Henry lunges at Gallows with his cutlass. Gallows strikes back.

Just then, Skullcap and the other pirates storm the deck, their swords and cutlasses raised. "Mutiny!" they shout. They'd planned to stop Captain Gallows from stealing the treasure, but they didn't count on finding him pinned to the ropes by another pirate captain.

"Light the arrows!" Gallows gasps. "Set Heinous Henry's ship afire!"

"No!" I shout. "There are people on that ship."

"Pirates, lad," Gallows chuckles. "Not people."

"Don't do it, Gallows," Heinous Henry says. "We're carrying black powder on that ship and—"

But Captain Gallows repeats his order. "Fire!"

"—our hold is filled—"

Before anyone can stop them, Jolly and Roger send a barrage of fire arrows zooming across the water.

"—with—"

## BOOM!

Smoke, masts, cannons, ropes, and barrels burst into the air above the Salish Sea. And thousands of... brown balls?

"Ow!" Captain Gallows screams as the balls rain down on his sweaty head.

"—potatoes," Heinous peeps. "We was just coming from picking up a load from Salt Spring Island. Salt Spring potatoes are the best. It's the springwater of course that makes them so delicious—"

"Ow! Ow! Owoo!" Gallows hollers. "I'll take anything—*anything*—but spuds!"

CHAPTER NINE

It turns out that no pirates died when the *Diabla Maria* exploded. They were all in a dinghy, rowing toward our ship. As the potatoes crashed down, they snuck over the side and brandished their swords.

The fighting erupted in a blaze of blades. ZING! ZANG! SMACK! Meringue joined in, fighting for both sides, pulling the pirates' hair and flapping her wings in their faces. CAW!

"You've got treasure aboard," Heinous Henry growled as he and Gallows crossed swords. "Why else would you turn tail when you saw our ship?"

"I never saw your ship!"

"Wait!" I yell to Heinous Henry and his crew. "It's true! He turned the ship around because there's treasure down here. Enough for everyone."

Skullcap pauses from squashing a pirate's nose with a spatula. "It's true."

"Gallows was going to take it for himself," I explain.

"He was, eh?" asks one of Heinous Henry's pirates with palm trees tattooed all over him. "The name's Palm," he tells me.

"He wasn't even going to tell his own crew," I say.

The pirates turn on Gallows. Within minutes, both he and Heinous Henry are strapped to the mizzenmast.

"What did *I* do?" Heinous Henry blubbers.

"For one thing, you left an innocent baby to die," Peggy says.

"Yeah, that was mean," grunts Cut-Purse. "Even for a pirate."

"What about me? I *saved* the baby!" Gallows whinges. "I held him for an hour, clucking at him. Then I laid him gently on a farmhouse doorstep with a note."

His words shoot through me like lightning. "A n-note?" I stammer.

"Yeah, a note. I can write a little, okay? I can even do a little calligraphy."

"D-did you wrap the baby in a green h-hat?"

Gallows squints his one eye. "I did."

"And whittle a pin to affix the note?"

"How do you know all this, boy?"

I run to the galley and, moments later, drop the hat and pin at the captain's bound feet. "This is how I know."

One Ear studies the pin. "This is the captain's work, all right. This notch here is like his signature—he adds it to everything he carves."

"Captain Gallows," I say. "I'm the baby you saved that day."

Gallows's one eye goes wide. "Blow me down! So you are. I thought I recognized that heart-shaped face and rose-red lips. That sweet thatch of black hair. Bet your earlobes are still soft as butter..."

"Honestly, Gallows," One Ear hisses.

Heinous stares at me like he's seen a ghost. His eyes fill with tears. "I'm sorry," he snuffles. "I try not to be so bad."

"Don't believe him," Palm says. He pulls an onion from Heinous Henry's collar. "Here's where his tears come from. Waves it under his eyes whenever he wants something. Who's the cook on this ship?"

"Skullcap," I say.

Skullcap shakes his head. "Not me. The boy's the real cook."

"Do something useful with this, a'right?" Palm tosses the onion my way. I catch it!

The ship tilts as a wave rolls under us. Hundreds of potatoes tumble portside.

We tell Heinous Henry's pirates about the pollock swallowing jewels and how there's probably a treasure chest right below us. I tell them that Gallows and One Ear were lowering me in the net to get it.

"A skinny lad like you? You would have frozen to death!" Palm shakes a finger at Captain Gallows. "You dog! You would have killed the same boy whose life you saved."

"I say two of us go down, one from each ship," Skullcap suggests. "That way we keep it equal. Who can swim?"

No one raises a hook.

"Okay, then, who wants to be covered in pig grease and lowered in the net?"

Every hook shoots up.

As Heinous Henry and Captain Gallows struggle against their ropes, Cut-Purse and one of Heinous Henry's pirates slather pig fat on their bodies for insulation, and we lower them into the bracing Salish Sea.

The first time the two come up, they've got three rubies from the ocean floor. The second time up, they've got emeralds plus a few pollock that got caught up in their net. And they've seen a treasure chest. Third time up, their gold teeth chatter, but in their arms is the treasure chest, its lid painted with pretty flowers.

As the pirates divvy up the rubies, emeralds, and diamonds, inventing stories about how it got to the bottom of the sea, I shovel potatoes into cooking pots and boil up a potato-pollock bisque, lightly flavoured with onion. The pirates eat every last bit, then arm wrestle for who gets to lick the spoon.

After a lot of burping, the pirates raise their glasses of grog. "Here's to the galley boy!"

"To the laddie!"

"What is your name, anyway?" Palm asks.

"I don't know," I say.

"How about Rubyheart?" Skullcap suggests.

"Aye! Here's to Pirate Rubyheart!" the pirates cheer.

I like the name. It's better than Kitch. But I still want my own name. My real name. It's out there somewhere. I know it.

All evening, the pirates play cards, dance jigs, and count their booty.

I clutch my full purse tightly in my hand.

At midnight, when the full moon is overhead, the pirates bundle Heinous and Gallows into a dinghy along with loyal One Ear, fifty pounds of tack, and three barrels of drinking water. They shoot off three cannons and shout, "Good riddance!"

Meringue flaps and squawks after them until they're out of sight.

After we've hung our hammocks for the night, I present Skullcap with my green hat.

"For keeps?" he asks.

"To keep your ears warm."

"That's fine of you, Rubyheart."

"You've been kind to me," I say. "Thank you, Skullcap. Now that Gallows is gone, who will be the new captain?"

"We thought we'd run it together. Collectively. Make decisions as a group, by consensus.

And what will you, Rubyheart, do with your freedom?"

"Go to Salt Spring Island to look for my mother."

"I hope you find her, Rubyheart." Skullcap stretches out in his hammock. "It's my turn to sing tonight."

His voice is surprisingly lovely.

> But the best of friends must part
> Fair or foul the weather
> Hand yer flipper for a shake
> Now a song together
>
> Long we've tossed on the rolling main
> Now we're safe ashore
> Don't forget your old shipmate
> Fal dee ral dee doe!

As I drift off to sleep, Meringue ambles into the galley, flaps up to the hammock and settles herself by my head, cooing.

She's warm. And soft. As a feather pillow.

# An Interview with Sara Cassidy

Q: How did you come up with the idea for this book?

A: I was on a ship actually, a ferry that crosses the Salish Sea, outside, soaking up the summer light, sitting on top of a giant bin of lifejackets. Two kids ran past—even though you aren't supposed to run on deck. The one chasing the other shouted, "You!" The two looked like brothers, though—they both had thick curly hair and electric faces—so the chasing, shouting one would have known the other boy's name. Maybe his name was You, I thought. A boy named You. Or maybe, I mused, he was a boy without a name.

Then, as ocean air filled my nose, I started to wonder: *Could there be a boy without a name?*

Q: *Why did you decide to set the story on a pirate ship? What was your favourite part about writing the pirate characters?*

A: I wake up most mornings to the sound of a seagull's high-pitched whooping. The temperature is always cool in my neighbourhood because it is on the shore. Most of the air I breathe has galloped across the open sea from an unfathomable distance away, coming to a stop at my neighourhood's fences and front doors. I write in an upstairs room that has windows on all sides. I've thought of it as a crow's nest—the lookout at the top of a ship's mast. Also, I've always struck off on my own, even if it's been lonely at times. So it came naturally to set the story on a pirate ship.

The best part about pirates is they're ready for anything. They are an impulsive bunch, which makes them perfect for characters. They never say no. Unless you want them to do something dull. But you wouldn't want someone doing something dull in a book anyway.

Q: *Was it difficult to write a main character without a name? Did you think about giving him a name at any point while you were writing the story?*

A: No, I never did think about giving him a name. A name is like the Incredible Hulk's clothing. It lets us move and change beneath it. It's like water: never still, but constant. I really didn't want Main Character to take on a name that isn't his. His name is waiting for him somewhere, while he becomes who he fully is. Anyway, he gets temporary names, like Sweetheart, Kitch, Rubyheart, and Main Character, for shelter along the way.

Q: *Is the Salish Sea a real place, and are there really pirates there?*

A: The Salish Sea is a real place. It lies along the far west edge of Canada. It was taken over by violent, horrible, scary pirates (not a little bit funny) who named it for their king, a man named George. Georgia Strait, they called it. But then a group of the people who the pirates had been horrible to rose up and demanded the sea be named for them, people who boated and fished in the sea for thousands and thousands of years before the bloody pirates ever arrived. They are the Coast Salish people.

Q: *What are your plans for our hero? Are there more adventures awaiting him? Will he ever find out what* his real name is? And will we ever see the pirates from the Greasy Lobster and the Diabla Maria again?

A: There are indeed adventures awaiting our hero. He has so much to find, after all. I don't know if he will find out what his real name is—I can't see into the future. I am not sure if he will see the pirates from the *Greasy Lobster* or the *Diabla Maria* again in the flesh, but I do know that he will sing the songs he learned, that he will forever have a fondness for potato-onion bisque and porridge with raisins, and that he will never forget those foes, and friends.

**Sara Cassidy** has worked as a newspaper reporter and a tree planter in five Canadian provinces. Her fourteen books for young readers have received many honours including being short-listed for the Chocolate Lily Award, the Ruth and Sylvia Schwartz Children's Book Award, and the Bolen Books Children's Book Prize. Three are Junior Library Guild selections. Her poetry, fiction, and nonfiction for adults have been widely published. She lives in Victoria, British Columbia. For more information, visit saracassidywriter.com.

BILLIE WOODS

**Mike Deas** is an author/illustrator of graphic novels and books for young people, including *Dalen and Gole* and the *Graphic Guide Adventures* series. While he grew up with a love of illustrative storytelling, Capilano College's Commercial Animation Program helped Mike fine-tune his drawing skills and imagination. Mike and his family live on Salt Spring Island, British Columbia. For more information, visit deasillustration.com or follow him on Twitter @deasillos.